Mystery Of Spot's Missing Ball

Adam Hero

Archway Publishing books may be ordered through booksellers or by contacting:

Archway Publishing
1663 Liberty Drive
Bloomington, IN 47403
www.archwaypublishing.com
844-669-3957

ISBN: 978-1-6657-2863-8 (sc)
ISBN: 978-1-6657-2861-4 (hc)
ISBN: 978-1-6657-2862-1 (e)

Print information available on the last page.

Archway Publishing rev. date: 10/27/2023

To my daughter, Alivya (Liv), the love of my life! Daddy loves you.

On a cold, foggy, damp day, the puppy, Spot, woke up in a panic because he could not find his favorite missing squeaking tennis ball.

Spot thought to himself, *There could only be three possible suspects that would take my favorite ball; the crazy old lady next door, the big old grumpy dog on the other side of the fence or the sly, wise fox who lurks at nighttime.*

—Would you all like to help Spot look for clues to find out who stole his ball?

Spot takes his clue backpack and a flashlight to start investigating the backyard for clues. He notices something stuck in the bush flapping in the wind. So Spot walks up to the bush and finds a grey wig stuck in the branches and a cane on the ground next to the bush. Spot thinks to himself, *This has to be the crazy old lady's wig. How could it get stuck in my bush?*

Spot takes the wig and places it inside of his clue bag. Spot continues to search. He notices a fox trail going through the backyard leading to a hole under the shed and some fox fur on the ground. Spot thinks to himself, *It has to be that sneaky fox.*

As Spot is following the trail he finds a pile of drool and a collar with the name "Theo" on it. *That means the big old grumpy dog was in my yard!*

—What could he have been doing in Spot's yard?

Spot has now found some clues;
the grey wig, a cane, fox trail, fox
fur, pile of drool, and a dog collar.

—Who do you think took Spot's favorite
ball? Everyone write down their answer.

_____

_____

_____

Time for Spot to go speak to the suspects. Spot first goes to visit Theo. Spot barks to get Theo's attention. He then asks, "Why is your collar and drool in my yard?"

Theo responds, "That dang fox was at it again, trying to steal my all-gold name-tag. So I dug under the fence to chase him down, but as I got the fox in my mouth, he scratched my tongue and got away too fast under the shed."

Spot asks, "Did you see a tennis ball?"

Theo says, "No! Now give me my collar before you are my new chew toy!"

Spot thinks, *If the fox was out stealing last night, it must have been him.* Spot barks into the fox hole. The fox comes out. The fox says, "Why do you bother me while I rest?"

Spot says, "I heard you were out stealing last night. Give me my ball back!"

Fox explains, "The ball was next on my list, but that grumpy Theo slobbered all over me. So I had to cut the night short and take a shower. Now let me be." The fox says to Spot. As Spot leaves he notices the fox has a pair of old-lady glasses.

Spot grabs the glasses and goes to the crazy old lady's house. Spot knocks. The lady shouts, "I'm not buying any chocolate! Leave me alone!"

Spot says, "I'm not selling anything. It's me, the puppy across the street. I have found your glasses. Fox stole them!" Spot gives the old lady her glasses.

Spot peeks into her house and notices a basket of tennis balls. Spot thinks to himself, *These must be other puppies tennis balls.* Spot says, "Hey lady, I know you're crazy, but why must you steal puppies' toys?"

The old lady is very confused and does not know what Spot is talking about.

The old lady says, "Those are rotten apples. I went out last night and gathered apples off the ground to make my homemade, famous, rotten-apple pie. Then a big dog ran by and knocked my wig right off of me."

Spot puts his paw to his face and shakes his head. Spot jumps up in the air and puts the glasses on the old lady's face. The old lady chuckled to herself. She couldn't believe she thought tennis balls were apples!

Spot jumps into the basket and starts digging for his favorite ball. He hears a squeak and cannot stop wagging his tail. Spot found his ball!

Spot returns to his dog house and thinks, *What a crazy morning that was.*

OK, how many readers thought it was the crazy old lady? Reveal your answer.

Author Biography

Delightful, charming, witty, funny and an uncanny flare to write a children's mystery book. Adam includes his character traits to his writing!

To read more about Adam's bio, visit Mystery of Spot's Missing Ball on social media sites.

Printed in the United States
by Baker & Taylor Publisher Services